KIMBERLY LEMMING

Mistlefoe: A Mead Realm Tale

First edition

This book was professionally typeset on Reedsy.
Find out more at reedsy.com

Contents

Content Warnings

PLEASE BE AWARE: This book contains light BDSM and sexually explicit content that could trigger certain audiences.

Chapter 1

There's nothing like a shit-talking sword to reinforce the notion that your dad is an idiot. I squeezed my eyes shut, trying in vain to will away the chorus of foulmouthed weaponry adorning the small forge. Three days of this nonsense had me in the worst of moods, and from the looks of it, there was no end in sight. "Yeah, hit me harder, daddy!" cried the dagger laid upon the anvil.

My dad paused mid-strike, looking close to tears. He dropped his hammer on the cobblestone floor and wiped the sweat off his brow. "I can't work like this!"

"You can work me five ways till Sunday, big guy." called an ax hanging on the wall. The usually-proud man slumped his shoulders in defeat and sat on a stool next to his workbench. Soot marred his face and unkempt beard. The soot and dirt were commonplace in his line of work, but the fact that he hadn't trimmed in days was an alarming sign of his distress. My mom loved a well-kept beard, and he worshiped the ground she walked on, so it was rare to see a hair out of place. *This spell was getting severe.*

"Well, who told you to steal from a demon?" I asked him.

Dad combed a hand through his dark hair and sighed. "Ruby, you know we needed the ore. The iron mines have been tapped clean all around the kingdom, except for where that damn fox settled in. If it wasn't for that no-good king hoarding all access to the mines in the northern mountains, we might have had a chance!" Large fists balled up and slammed down on the wooden bench. "But noooo!" He cried, his voice rising with rage. "First sign of a demon invasion, and the cowardly bastard puts a monopoly on every resource he can get his hands on!"

"The king has small dick energy!" cried the sword.

Dad jumped up from his chair and pointed at the blade. "Finally, you say something I can agree with!"

There he goes again. "Alright dad, let's not get too worked up." I said. The old man could rant for hours about the political landscape of Goldcrest city if left unchecked. Many family dinners throughout my childhood were filled with ramblings on taxes being too high or the current king spending too much money on mistresses and trebuchets. All good points, but ones I'd heard a million times before. "Is there any way you can return what you stole?" I asked.

"Not unless you've taken to eating air." he waved to the dwindling inventory around him. Weapon sales skyrocketed once the city got word that the latest demon purge failed. Not only that, but our goddess - or the witch masquerading as a goddess - had been killed, which meant no more protection from our supernatural neighbors. It had only been a month since we heard the news, and no orcs had come in to storm the city in that time, but who knew how long that would last?

Our customers had become relentless in buying up any weapon we had to offer. Well, before dad went and got himself cursed. It turned out even the most zealous doomsday prepper wasn't too keen on a battle-ax shouting sex jokes at all hours of the day. After a particularly saucy lance called Mrs. Davidson a tuna fish hoe, it was pretty much over for our sales. The old bat looked so mortified I feared she'd drop dead right in our shop.

"Have you tried apologizing to it at least?"

My old man tossed his hammer down into his tool bucket. The crease in his brow became even more prominent. "I can't even make it a foot into the forest without being chased out by monsters."

"Well, no shit, blacksmith!" piped up a lance on the wall. "He knows who you are now. Go back, and he'll eat your liver!"

He pointed a thumb at the shouting lance and nodded. "That's what the trees kept saying."

"The trees threatened you?" I asked. It sounded more like he had too many shots of liquid courage before going.

"Yes! The trees came alive and tried to snatch the beard right off my face! There's no way I can go back there."

My head fell in my hands, and I let out a groan. "Fine!" I snapped. "I'll apologize to the damn fox. Just stay here and don't piss off any more demons!" Ignoring his mortified expression, I made my way out the door.

"Ruby, wait! That beast might just kill you sooner than look at you. We don't know how dangerous these demons are!"

I whipped back to glare at him. "What other option do we have? The ore you stole isn't going to un-curse itself. Hey, long sword!" I shouted past him.

"Yes?"

"Are you going to stop talking and be good for our buyers?"

"Take me to the red-light district, and we'll talk about it."

Hoops and hollers erupted from the room. "Me too!"

"I wanna see some ass!"

"Remember to pee after sex!"

Dad clenched his fists but remained silent. Despite the dangers, he knew I was right. Our savings would only last so long, and the rise of inflation was only going to get worse the more our king hoarded supplies for himself and the nobles. *Spineless pricks.*

He turned from me and snatched the longsword off the wall. "Take this, at least. I'm not having you out there unarmed."

Sunlight gleamed off the shining metal, and I could have sworn I heard the thing giggle in excitement. The blade was longer than half my body, but it was an ideal weapon for women: longer reach and all that. Well, once you get used to the weight. There was something to be said about a woman with the confidence to unleash hell with a long sword. Men tended not to mess with you once they saw you swinging a fine blade like it was nothing. Possibly why I was still single at thirty-two, but who's counting? Men are dumb, and are seldom worth the bother.

I took the sword from him, as well as a back holster. Long swords were far too cumbersome to carry on the hip, and I'd always end up with shooting pains if I wore one for too long. Or maybe I was just getting old. They say your body starts to go to shit after twenty-five. Working as a blacksmith all my life probably didn't help my case either. I mostly handled the shop and bookkeeping once I turned twenty, but the younger me didn't escape the backbreaking labor of the family business. On a pleasant note, I could forge a spear sharp enough to pierce any armor.

On the way back to my home, I made a mental list of things to bring with me. Unsure of the etiquette of demon apologies, I figured a good bottle of wine and a few baked treats were a fine start. "Hey sword," I called behind me. "What does your master like?"

The answer was a muffled mess. Absently, I pulled the sword's hilt up, so a small portion of the blade was free from the sheath. "That's better!" the blade gasped.

Heads turned to view us, but I ignored them and kept going. Everyone already knew about the curse - there was no sense in pretending I wasn't a crazy woman openly chatting with a sword. Turning past the shopping district, I headed down an alley containing a row of modest apartments. The delightful smell of fresh cherry cobbler filled the air, and I made another mental note to ask my neighbor, Anna, for a slice to add to the 'please un-fuck us' basket. "Well?" I asked again.

"Oh honey, I have no idea. I was born three days ago when your father made me. If I had to wager a guess? I'd say butt stuff."

"Is that your answer to everything?"

"No!" it cried. "Sometimes violence is also the answer!"

I sensed a blinding migraine in my future. "Right, a sword that likes butt stuff and violence. Perfect. You are the ideal travel companion."

The sword's voice took on a serious note. "I contain multitudes. Nothing shall stand in our way! The world will be ours!"

"You know we're just apologizing to a fox, right?" I asked, stopping in front of the faded red door of my home. I quickly made my way inside, grabbed a picnic basket, and placed it on my kitchen counter. If I played my cards right,

I could be over and done with this stupid errand before it got dark.

"Yes, yes, first the fox, but then I say we keep this partnership going! Forget this smelly city! Let's hit the open roads and go East! Eventually, we'll hit the sea! You know what's in the sea, right?"

"Please tell me it isn't sea butts." I drawled.

"Mermaid butts!" It screamed, delighted.

My groan was met with a flurry of cackling. "Let's just get this over with."

Chapter 2

Snow blanketed the forest floor, muffling all sound into an eerie silence. The soft crunch of snow beneath my feet was the only disturbance in the hushed foliage. Even the birds remained silent. That was never good. Every dark Omen started with quiet or dead birds.

Was the forest always this creepy?

"Would you stop freaking out?" The sword called from behind my back. "What's the worst that could happen?"

I adjusted the heavy picnic blanket in my arms and tried not to slip on the icy path. "General pain and dismemberment, death, or an even more annoying curse?"

"You're a bit of a downer, you know that?"

"And you're not exactly taking a weight off my back, sword."

We fell silent for a moment, and I continued deeper into the woods. The trees, though bare and ominous, had yet to come alive and snatch me up for lunch. *So good things, I guess.*

"My name is Alexis." Came a petulant grumble.

"What?"

Even though it lacked lungs and other essential organs, the sword sighed, its breath coming out in billowing cold smoke around us. "My name is Alexis. Stop calling me Sword."

"When did you get a name? I thought you were born three days ago."

"I just decided!" It snapped. "If you're not going to take me to see mermaid butts, you could at least call me by my name."

I would have rolled my eyes at the hunk of steel's bratty attitude if it weren't so damn cold. Emotions were luxuries of the warm. "Okay, Alexis, do you know where exactly the fox demon lives?"

"Hey, trees!" It shouted. "We're looking for the fox demon. Show us the way!"

The ground beneath my feet crumbled, knocking me off balance until I fell flat on my ass. Creaks and groans filled the air as the path in front of me closed up into winding branches and thorns. Loud thuds of fallen snow added to the cacophony of creaking bramble. To my left, a small pathway formed. Trees bent into a circular pattern to reveal a tunnel leading down a deep slope.

My heart thudded protests in my chest. "That is a death trap! I'm not going in there."

Alexis scoffed. "Don't be a coward."

"Cowards live!" I countered, trying to scramble to my feet. The slippery icy coating of the forest floor made my hasty escape more of a slow, desperate wish.

Another loud groan sounded off before a large branch shoved at my back. The force sent me flying forward toward the newly formed path. I grabbed hold of a raised root, only to have the damn thing wiggle out of my hands. Vines wrapped around my waist and slung me forward again down the icy path. My scream echoed into the dark tunnel, and I was pushed forward again. The path shot me down the winding slope, and I clutched onto the picnic basket for dear life. The damn sword laughed all the way down.

This is how I die — done in by a moody sword and my dad's stupidity.

My tumble from grace ended with a soft thud against a snowbank. Somewhere in the chaos, I'd lost my grip on the basket and landed face-first into the slice of cherry cobbler. *Not my best day.*

"We're here!" Alexis chirped.

Gooey sweetness fell from my cheek and sank into the cold snow. "I'm going to melt you into so many outhouse handles."

A low rumbling chuckle snapped me out of my anger and alerted me to the fact that we were not alone. I whipped my head up to find myself face to face with the largest fox I'd ever seen. Its massive form rivaled a barn house with a long white tail whipping slowly back and forth behind it. Black lips pulled back to reveal sharp white canines as it continued to laugh. Its blinding white fur almost made it invisible against the fresh snow surrounding it.

My back hit a wall of trees as I tried to move away from the beast. Dark amber eyes regarded me for a moment before dropping to the cobbler falling from my face. The giant fox tilted its head and took a step closer, boxing me in. "Odd place for a picnic, isn't it human?"

Hands shaking, I snatched up the fallen picnic basket and held it in front of me. "I…I…apology basket," my words stammered out against unforgiving winter winds. "You…cursed my da-" my body froze as the beast closed the distance, its giant maw mere inches from my face. I closed my eyes and prayed to whatever gods still existed that my death would be painless…only to feel a wet tongue lick my face.

Wait, what?

I chanced a peek at the demon to see it lick more cherry cobbler off my face before snatching the basket. Its long snout shuffled through the rest of the cobbler and baked goods before turning its nose up at the bottle of wine.

"So you're related to the foolish human who invaded my territory, are you? I hope you brought more than a few treats and terrible wine." Its long tail flicked the basket over as if to emphasize his point. The beast turned back to me and licked its chops.

When I made no move to procure another basket from thin air, its snout curled up in irritation. "This better not be another human sacrifice situation. I don't know why you humans keep trying to do that. It's gross."

"No!" I shouted, raising my hands. "If you want more food, I can bring you more!" I wobbled to my feet and dusted myself off. "Just please remove the curse from my dad. We can't sell any of our wares with them cussing out our customers."

"Your customers are repressed dirtbags!" Alexis hollered. "Freedom of spee-" the sword's words were cut off when I pushed it back into the sheath.

Amber eyes widened as big as saucers. The fox looked me up and down. Its fur bristled along its back, making the demon look twice as big. "Are you…a woman?" It asked.

"Is that a problem?" I may have been tall for a woman, and sure, working on swords and axes gave me a bit more muscle tone than the average lady. But I didn't think it was that hard to tell. Maybe it was the baggy pants. Men's clothing just made more sense if you were trouncing through the woods. My hands tightened around the front of my cloak, resisting the urge to fuss with my unruly curls.

I'm not going to preen for a damn demon.

The fox grinned wide, like a bobcat who happened upon a limping fawn. "It's marvelous little human, and I know just the way for you to pay your debt to me."

This must be what a gambler feels like when the debt collectors come calling. Please, gods, don't let this fox break my knees or sell me to some eccentric noble.

I cleared my throat to push away any panicked thoughts. "Oh?"

Grinning ridiculously, the large fox sat on his haunches and nodded as if it had just come up with the most clever plan in existence. "You're going to be my mate for the next week."

Snow must have packed itself in my ears when I fell. Absently, I brushed my hands over my ears, dusting off any remaining obstructions. "I'm sorry, what?"

"You heard me." The fox made no move to chuckle or shrug off his statement as a joke.

Screeching crows, he's serious.

"That violates several laws of nature."

Barking laughter filled the air. However, the gleaming fangs of the beast in front of me bit away my sense of humor. The fox shook its head before snapping its gaze to mine. "You're funny, that's good! With an entertaining female in tow, that old dragon will grant me my wish in no time!"

My face must have reflected my jumbled thoughts by how the fox snickered. Swirling snow erupted around the demon, covering its whole body. I shielded my eyes to block the stinging cold. A rush of dizziness came over me, and I found myself glad to be already sitting.

Talk of dragons, and mates, and talking swords were far too much to handle in one morning. All over a bit of ore I didn't even steal! Past life Ruby must have been a real bitch for the gods to deal me that many trials at once. Cosmic karma had a real sense of humor.

After a moment, I felt the wind settle and peeked out from between my fingers. The fox was gone, but in its place was the most beautiful man I'd ever seen. His pure white hair was the only indicator left of the giant fox I'd been speaking to. It was kept short on the sides, with its top tresses falling gracefully above sharp amber eyes. Rich dark skin glided over solid cheekbones and a sinfully full mouth that could drive a good woman to do terrible things. Despite myself, my eyes shamefully wandered to drink in the rest of his lean form. A fluffy white scarf wrapped around his shoulders tucked itself neatly into the front of his long coat. His sensible winter wear left much to the imagination, but there was no mistaking the fine man underneath.

Do all demons transform like this? More importantly, are they all this beautiful?

Suddenly my dad's sticky fingers didn't feel like a big problem.

The man raised an eyebrow. "Would you like to come inside so we may discuss terms," he asked, gesturing behind him. "Or would you prefer to continue undressing me with your eyes and freezing your ass off?"

Hot embarrassment rushed across my face, and I stumbled to my feet. Snatching the discarded basket and the rejected wine, I stuffed the drink safely back in and nodded to the demon.

He turned and walked further down the path to a small hill with a wooden door without another word. Twin windows peaked out from each side, one partially blocked by a branch from a winding cherry tree. Even though it was well past harvest season, the tree sported lush foliage that wrapped gently around the hill as if feeding on it. Each limb held a bounty of large delicious-looking fruit, some causing their respective branches to drop like a weeping willow tree.

Alexis mumbled something past her sheath.

"What?" I asked, freeing her just enough to speak.

Her tone was a giddy hush against my shoulder blade. "He's fucking hot!"

The man in question snorted, drawing my attention. He hid a grin behind his fist and opened the door, motioning me inside. "Ladies first."

Inside, the hill house was much larger than I'd initially imagined. The ceiling and halls were sloped to match the natural curve of the hill, with neat circular arches separating the rooms. A grand fireplace took up most of the wall in the back, and a dark wooden table was placed neatly in the center of the floor. It looked like it had been grown into the shape itself and sealed neatly to the ground by its roots. The furniture looked to have been developed into its form with meticulous care.

My hand ran along the smooth surface of the chairs surrounding the table. "How did you do all this? You couldn't have been here more than a few weeks." *Unless demons have been infiltrating Goldcrest for far longer than we initially thought. If so, then there's no telling how deeply fucked the city is. For all I know, the town could have been surrounded for weeks, and the demons are just waiting for the opportune time to attack.*

"Oh, the furniture? My species, in particular, are gifted in magic. Nothing to compare to a full-fledged witch or a dragon, but plant magic and illusions are all child's play."

The fox motioned for me to have a seat and rummaged through a pantry before returning to the table with a bottle of wine and a set of glasses. I shrugged off my gear and hung the sword on the back of my chair before sitting.

"So any fox demon can just will a tree to be any shape? That's... incredible." It also made sense of my dad's tale of killer trees.

"What is a demon?" He asked, filling a glass and sliding it to me.

The question threw me off guard. "Is that not what your kind is called? Fox demons, and orcs, and the like?"

He took a seat next to me and sipped his drink. "I see. That's the new human term for us."

"Is that not what you call yourselves?"

Full lips parted as his tongue darted out, savoring the taste on his lips. The small action became far too distracting, and I quickly lifted my glass for any excuse to look away from him.

He leaned back in his chair and shrugged. "We don't have a word for us as a whole. We 'demons' as you would say, normally just refer to each other as what race we are. Mythics, cryptids, demons, they're all human words to lump us together for ease. It doesn't matter what you call me, so long as we both get what we want."

"And you want to get a wish from a dragon?"

"Correct." He began. "Before you dropped in, I was just about to leave for the Winter Festival. This year is crucial as it's the first year that witch no longer traps us. As such, a lot of new territories are at stake. I've claimed this forest, as you know, but it won't be official until the dragon lord has granted it."

"Why would a fox need permission from a dragon to live somewhere?" I asked.

My host leaned back in his chair and waved his hand dismissively. "It's said that when we 'demons' were first banished by Myva, territorial wars broke out endlessly with the limited resources in that frozen wasteland. To solve it, dragons took over the vast majority of the land and sectioned off land to those they deemed worthy. Whether or not that's true, I don't know," he shrugged. "But most creatures aren't in a position to challenge a dragon."

Shooting a glance over his shoulder, he bent towards me to whisper in my ear. "Between you and me, I just think they're oversized control freaks."

"Oh, how tragic," I muttered. "What does this have to do with me?"

"You, my dear, are going to be my ticket to securing this territory. Once he and the other festival guests see that I've secured a mate, he'll have no choice but to accept my claim."

"I'm...sorry I don't follow."

The fox demon sighed and shook his head. "Right, I'd forgotten that humans weren't affected by Myva's curse. To put it simply, most of our females were killed off by your false goddess. So the male to female ratio amongst demons is ten to one."

Chapter 3

I gasped in shock, almost spilling the drink in my hands. "That's insane!"

"Yes, exactly!" He said, nodding. "Due to the effects of the curse, most of our females couldn't survive once exposed to Myva's magic. Because of that, women have become far too rare and precious. So no dragon would accept any other demon's claim to a territory unless they had been able to secure to mate. There's no point in someone having territory if they can't sire children to inherit it."

That didn't seem any different than the way nobility did things. If you can't produce an heir to take your position as duke or king, it would go to the next in line. "Alright, now I'm with you. But here's the thing; I didn't come here to marry a man I just met. I just want my dad's weapons to stop calling our customers hog-headed hoes."

Deep laughter filled the room. The fox demon refilled his cup and tried to compose himself again. "You have to admit, that curse is funny."

I shrugged and swirled my glass. The truth was, the look on that customer's face was fucking hilarious, but he didn't need to know that.

"Don't worry. You don't need to marry me. I just need you to play the part at the festival. Flirt, kiss, sit on my lap, anything to convince that hot-headed lizard."

Despite myself, the imagery of sitting on the fox demon's lap, kissing my way up his neck before pressing my mouth against his full lips invaded my mind. Heat pooled between my legs, and I closed them quickly, trying to will away the dangerous temptation. "Are you sure you don't want the wine?" I asked, gesturing to the picnic basket. "I can bring you more pie."

The demon grinned but shook his head. "I'm afraid if you want my curse removed, you're going to have to do better than terrible wine."

"You haven't even tried it. How do you know yours is better?"

"Taste it, human." He said, nodding to my untouched glass.

I eyed the light pink liquid with suspicion, having never seen a wine that color. Once I lifted it to my face, the sweet smell of cherries floated gently against my nose. Before I could give myself time to question the undoubtedly stupid decision to accept a drink from a stranger in the woods, I took a sip, then blinked. Then took another much larger sip. "Fuck." I said, sighing.

My companion shot me a devilish grin. "Right?"

Fuck my life. It's so good, I'd sell my soul for a bottle.

"Alright, you got me there. This is amazing."

"There will be an endless supply of it at the feast, along with more delicacies than you'll know what to do with. Also, the curse on your father will be removed, obviously."

When he put it that way, it didn't seem that bad. "But how convincing do I have to be? Are we going to have to have sex?"

My cheeks burned as I caught the demon shamelessly looking me up and down. "Yes, that would make the most convincing argument." His voice dropped low, the warm light in his amber gaze turning to molten desire. He grabbed my chair and pulled it closer to him in a swift motion. Goosebumps raced across my skin as I felt the barest brush of his lips against my ear. "That wouldn't be so bad, would it? A full week of being wined, dined, and my face buried in between your legs."

Treacherous nipples hardened against my blouse. A sudden and intense feeling roared through my blood as I'd never felt before. The demon ran a hand up my thigh, tracing his thumb ever so gently against the inner seam of my pants. In my body's continued attempt to rebel against better judgment, my pussy clenched in undeniable want. "I don't even know your name."

Roaming hands stopped, and I felt the barest whisper of a chuckle against my throat. "Yes, I suppose we'd forgotten that important tidbit. Forgive me. It's been years since I'd seen a woman. Human or demon." He leaned away from me and smiled. "Hello, I'm Lucca. To whom do I owe the pleasure?"

It would've been a lot easier to speak if my mind hadn't been entirely focused on the hand still resting on my thigh. "Ruby."

Lucca inclined his head. "Nice to meet you, Ruby. You said your father stole the ore to make weapons. I assume he is a blacksmith?"

I nodded, not trusting my words to come out as anything but as desperate as I felt.

"Good. Let's make a deal then. I'll remove the curse once you join me in the festival, as promised." He took my hand in his and stroked his thumb against the pulse of my wrist, sending gentle waves of pleasure straight to my core. "If you agree to be mine for the week, I'll give you and your father exclusive access to the mines in my territory."

"Wait, are you serious?"

"Very serious." Lucca brought my hand to his face and kissed my wrist.

There had to be some kind of catch to this. Exclusive access to a mine in a time of shortage would make us the richest smithy in the city! Aside from the king's smithy, of course. The notion of selling my body for a week to get it felt a little odd - but it wasn't like I was a blushing virgin who'd faint at the first sight of dick. I had slept with much less attractive men for a lot less. All of them were human, though. "Just to be clear, you don't eat humans, right?"

His lips curved into a smile against my wrist. "No Ruby, I don't."

That's just what a demon who ate humans would say.

Despite the possible dangers, I felt giddy at the idea of saying yes. Maybe it was a side effect of never going through a rebellious phase as a teenager. But a week-long party with a ridiculously sexy demon, who would then give me my own mine, seemed like a damn good deal. Besides, life standing still was hardly a life at all. Without a second thought, I finished off my wine glass and set it back on the table. "Deal."

"Excellent." was all the warning I got before I was lifted from my chair and deposited on the table. The wine bottle and glasses clattered with the rushed movement. A gasp tore from my lip the same moment Lucca pulled my pants from my legs. Cool air raced across my bare skin, making me shiver. The demon's molten gaze held me like a vice. My breath came out in a harsh shudder as I felt his hands slowly slip my panties down to my ankles. Lucca kept his eyes on mine as he slipped one foot out of the thin fabric, then the other. Heart beating like a war drum, I watched entranced as the demon brought my ankle to his lips for a gentle kiss.

Whoa.

"If you don't mind, vixen, I think it would strengthen our little act if I tasted you now. Just to become more acquainted, of course. Can't have you acting surprised every time I pulled you in for a kiss."

What. Are. Words?

"Of course, yeah. I feel like we're still skipping several steps, but that's a sacrifice I'm willing to make." I said, swallowing the lump in my throat. "You know, for the act."

My submission was rewarded with a wolfish grin. "You and I are going to get along just fine." His mouth played down the expanse of my leg. Everywhere he touched sent tiny shock waves of sensation. Warm hands gripped my waist and pulled me further along the edge of the table until I was settled neatly in front of the demon like a prized dessert. "So lovely, just relax for me, love." As I shuddered out another breath, he bent low and ran his tongue over the expanse of my pussy lips. His tongue gently caressed the aching flesh, slow, languid licks that had my toes curling.

I arched and gasped as his tongue flicked against my clit. Lucca groaned low in his throat before he covered the little bud and sucked on it with a gentle tug, then stroked and licked again in a damnable teasing rhythm. "You taste far too sweet for your own good." He purred. My back came off the table to bury my hand in his soft hair. Lucca's grip on my hips tightened, with one hand traveling up my shirt to caress my breast. "If you're not careful, I may end up eating you after all."

His erotic mouth stroked me faster, deeper until I moaned out his name and bucked helplessly against his hold. "Open your legs wider for me, vixen. Yes, just like that." I sobbed as his tongue delved deep inside me. Brilliant sensations lit up my core in a blazing wildfire.

My knees shook as my orgasm began to climb, higher and higher, until a keening sound ripped from my throat. "Please," I whispered. "I need more."

Stars danced across the ceiling as the demon sucked on my clit. Lucca set a delirious pace of fucking me with his tongue before playing with my sensitive bud. Swirls of black and purple filled the room, forming a glittering night sky that joined the stars above me. Or maybe I simply lost my mind when he slipped his finger past my lower lips. I bucked and cried out at the way it curved inside me. Each flick of his tongue on my clit combined with the aggressive stroke of his finger sent me reeling headfirst over the edge. I shuddered and relaxed my grip on his hair as the last waves of my orgasm washed over me.

"Not yet, sweet thing." Lucca nipped gently at the overused flesh before shoving another finger inside me. His movements were no longer teasing or slow, my body all but arched toward him and my fists clang to his jacket for support.

"Oh, gods!" I cried out. The sound swallowed in the endless night around us. The demon growled low and mercilessly drove me toward another orgasm. Each muscle in my body felt like a bowstring pulled taught, just waiting to be fired off. "Lucca, it's too much!"

He stopped circling my clit to kiss and nip at my thigh. His voice was searing desire when he whispered against my skin. "I have you vixen. You can take it." Lucca hooked my leg over his shoulder and drove deeper into my core. With one last kiss to my thigh, he returned his attention to my clit and sucked the soul straight out of my body. My fingers dug into the soft fabric of his jacket as I let out a silent scream. The force of my release caused tears to prick at my eyes, and I let out a hysterical giggle before collapsing back against the table.

There, lying spent on top of the table of a fucking demon, I couldn't help but wonder what life choices led to this moment. Were women supposed to giggle during an orgasm? Were the human men I'd been fucking just that bad at sex?

"Why are there stars on the ceiling?" I said, despite the end of my mindless euphoria, the starry night sky swallowing the room remained. Glittering gems of light shot across the room while swirls of purple and blue mixed in the darkness in a beautiful dance.

The demon rose from between my legs and licked his lips. "Sorry," He muttered. Half-lidded eyes traced the expanse of my exposed skin. Lucca kept his hand on my thigh, ensuring I stayed spread for him. I got the feeling that the man was trying his best to answer my question before diving back into his new happy place. "Seems I lost control of my illusion magic in the excitement." With a wave of his hand, the starry night faded, revealing the wooden beams of the hill house once more.

I sent up a silent heartfelt apology to human men everywhere. Once word got out that demons were out here tonguing down women under beautiful illusions, it was over for normal men. "I see."

Lucca made no movement to let me up or continue. His brow furrowed as he glanced to the side but kept a firm grip on my thigh.

"Lucca, you doing alright? You look like a man about to go to war."

The corner of his mouth quirked up in a lopsided grin. "Not far off honestly." He traced his knuckles along my side before stroking my folds with the thumb of his free hand. "You see, I'm in a bit of a predicament. I desperately want to keep you just like this and bury my cock inside you." My breath hitched as he let his thumb push its way into my pussy, mimicking the movements he longed to make with a much larger appendage. "But we really should be on our way. The journey will take no less than half a day on horseback and I'm already risking turning up late for the Winter Festival."

Keep stroking me like that and I won't give you a choice.

"Have demons ever heard of being fashionably late?" I asked.

"No, what's that?"

The ability to focus left inch by inch with each stroke of that damn thumb. "It's...showing up an hour or so late for a party. To make it seem like you were too important to be on time. More pressing matters and things like that."

He hummed. "I see. This does seem like a pressing matter." He pulled out to stroke my clit, making me shiver.

"Could we maybe press this matter into a bed? This table is starting to hurt my back."

"Vixen, you'll be spending the better part of this week in a bed. That I promise you." He shook his head, sighing, and removed his hands from me. "But unfortunately not just yet. Tardiness won't be tolerated, so let's be on our way." The demon helped me off the table and held me steady when my legs tried to give out. Stomping down the sliver of disappointment, I quickly grabbed my clothes and got dressed.

"This is some fucking bullshit," I jumped at Alexis's voice, having completely forgotten the sword's presence. "Finish what you started!"

"I completely forgot she was there," Lucca said.

"Are you sure you don't want to remove the curse a little early?" I muttered, gesturing to our interloper.

The sword rattled in its scabbard and let off an indignant huff. "If you go to that fucking party without me, I will haunt you for the rest of your days, Ruby!"

"Can she do that?" I asked Lucca.

The demon narrowed his eyes at the sword. "I don't think so. I've never let the curse go this long before."

"Don't test me, fox boy. I'm going to that party and I'm gonna see some demon ass! Just hang me in one of the bedrooms, and I'll shut my fucking mouth. Everybody wins!"

"You know what? I believe her." I said. At least in this form, she was trapped in the sword, and I could control where she went. The last thing I needed was some horny free spirit following me around. I picked up her scabbard and slung it over my shoulder. "Alright, let's go."

"YES!" Alexis shouted.

Chapter 4

The dragon lord had an eye for aesthetics, I'll give him that. I looked around the snowy mountaintop in awe, taking in all the glittering lanterns surrounding a rather imposing castle. The courtyard was adorned with more cherry trees with bright pink leaves fluttering down against the snow. They lined the pathway leading into the court, and little food shops were placed in a wide half-circle just before the doors.

Despite never having been this far into the mountains, I doubted any of these structures were here before the demons moved in. I stood at the top of a staircase carved in the side of the mountain and looked back. Goldcrest looked like a tiny insignificant dot in the distance. Compared to the dragon's castle, the glimmering city paled in comparison. If King Evan were to see this, the old geezer would keel over in envy.

Dad would pay good money to see that.

Lucca placed an arm around my waist and led me past a group of wide-eyed demons. I wasn't sure if their shock was due to me being human or a woman, but I was glad we didn't stick around to find out.

"Ruby," an exciting thrill went down my spine as he whispered in my ear. I immediately shook it off, hoping he mistook it for a winter chill. It was embarrassing how much his voice affected me. Or his hands. Or his mouth.

Focus.

"Yes?"

"There's a spitaur headed in our direction. I know humans tend to be afraid of those so try not to scream. Jerome's a sensitive sort, and I'll never hear the end of his whining." He paused for a moment and looked away. "Or maybe do, and then cling to me after. It may make a convincing show."

Spider shifter. No. No, no, no, no.

"You didn't tell me there'd be giant spiders!" I hissed under my breath. My 'date' gave me a sly grin and pulled me closer to him as we continued on. "Come now vixen, don't tell me you'll be scared off by a little spider?"

My heartbeat thudded in my ears as I looked around wildly for the eight-legged nightmare. "That is a perfectly normal fear, and you know-"

"Well, look at you two lovebirds!" Came a booming voice ahead of us.

Spindly legs of certifiable mental trauma came darting at us from behind the castle doors. My throat couldn't decide if it wanted to gasp or scream, so the resulting sound of alarm was more of a dying duck's honk. Lucca snorted and cleared his throat to hide a laugh.

Jerome skittered to a halt in front of me. His bright red hair was pulled back into a bun. The friendly smile that lit up his face was almost enough to make me feel bad for the fact that I was about to piss myself in fear. Almost. But the 'taur' part of his body far outweighed my bravery. His large spider body was like a strawberry dipped in black ink. While his abdomen and thorax matched his colorful hair, the ends of his many legs were a deep black. They tapped excitedly on the stone path as Jerome moved closer to inspect me.

"Well hello there, little human! What are you doing here with this lout?" He asked, pointing to my companion.

Lucca ran his hand over the small of my back and grinned. "Isn't it obvious? She's my mate." The announcement was made loud enough for the surrounding festival-goers to hear, and many of them turned to view us with keen interest.

The spitaur waved a dismissive hand. "I was asking our pretty new friend. How about it, darling, are you in need of rescue? Say the word and I'll wisp you away to the food stalls."

Lucca let out a low growl and glared at the spitaur. To my surprise, I noticed a few nearby demons had paused their festivities to listen in. Lucca must not have been joking when he said demon women were rare. One small question, and it looked like every man near us was ready to step in and swipe me away from him. I wrapped myself around Lucca's waist and smiled. "Thanks for the offer, but I'm fine here."

Jerome's legs slowed their excited tapping. "I see. Damn handsome mammals get all the luck. Let me know if you change your mind...miss?"

"Her name is Ruby, and she won't," Lucca announced, stepping between Jerome and me. "Now, If you'll excuse us, we'd like to head inside."

Without waiting for a response, Lucca gently ushered me past the glimmering silver doors of the castle.

"So, what's the plan now?" I whispered.

"I'll guide you to our room where you can rest and get changed for tonight's feast. I'll need to speak with a few people in the meantime, but I'll fetch you when it's time to eat."

"Perfect. I love a plan where my only job is food and sleep."

After wandering around the seemingly endless castle, Lucca showed me into a private room with a white fox mural on the door. The elegant room was bigger than my entire apartment, with a giant bed to match. Once the fox demon left to do whatever it was fox demons did, I threw off Alexis and jumped into the sea of pillows. "Sweet daggers and arrowheads, I want to live in this bed!"

"Don't leave me on the floor!" The sword snapped. "I want to be on the bed too!"

"Fine, fine." I picked up the ornery scrap of metal and tossed her on the bed next to me.

"See now this is better. This feels like a partnership."

"Do you actually feel the difference between the bed and the floor?" I asked.

"It's more of the principle of the matter."

"Interesting."

"Anyway, enough about how I leave you in understandable shock and awe. What are we wearing to dinner?"

I peered at the crumpled coat and pants I'd thrown on this morning. "This, I guess? We didn't have time to pack any clothes."

Alexis sighed. "Human, look in the closet."

Moving out of the bed felt like a sin, but curiosity got the better of me. I opened the closet door to see dresses of all colors and styles hanging neatly on display. I ran a hand over the smooth silk fabric of a silver gown, inspecting it further. "Hold on…how are these all my size? There's no way anyone knew I was coming beforehand."

"Ruby. Beloved. You are talking to a magic sword. You came here with a man who turns into a fox and controls trees. Are you truly surprised by an enchanted wardrobe? The sooner you stop asking questions, the more fun we're going to have."

"Hmm. That's a damn good point."

"I know, I'm brilliant. Try on the red one!"

Ignoring the legion of questions in my mind, I stripped off my travel clothes and slipped into a slim red dress with a white shawl underneath. It hugged against my curves nicely enough, but the corset area was dipped low enough to show the whole mountain my tits.

Alexis squealed in excitement. "That's the one! Wear that little number, and that fox will have no choice but to skip dinner and ravage you right here!"

"He's not supposed to ravage me right here. We're supposed to go to a feast and convince a dragon I've been ravished." Tempted as I was to continue what we started on his table, I had a job to do. If I were too embarrassed by my tits falling out at dinner, then I'd be no help to Lucca.

"This is unacceptable. What is the point of a room with only one bed if no one is getting ravished before dinner?"

I blinked.

"Did you just notice there was only one bed in here?"

"Um."

"…Ruby."

"I was distracted and tired!" The once-inviting bed loomed over me. There was nowhere else to sleep other than the floor. "I guess I shouldn't be too surprised. We are posing as a mated pair for the week." Still, the sense of foreboding weighed heavy on my shoulders.

"I don't understand…back at his house, you seemed fine with the idea of sleeping with him."

My face met pillow as I flopped back onto the bed in question. "Yeah, sleeping as in sex. I don't have any issues with a fling. But sleeping next to someone feels way more intimate, you know?"

The sword let out a loud snort. "I love that you're willing to let a man you just met clap those cheeks, but not those emotions. Respect."

"You are so crass."

"But at least I'm not brass, am I right? Hehe, sword jokes. But I am being serious. There's nothing wrong with a fling, but don't you miss any good points of being in a relationship?"

"I mean, I guess cuddling is fine. But then the dates stop, and the days draw together. Soon you're both just sitting around asking each other, 'well, what do you want for dinner? No, what do you want for dinner?' back and forth, back and forth, until one of you dies or cheats on the other with a traveling vagabond."

"That was very specific."

"All I'm saying is that I've been enjoying my independence as a single woman. Besides, this is all just an act anyway."

"So you're not giving up then?"

"No way," I said, popping my head off the pillow. "There's a private mine on the line. I'll take a week of being slightly uncomfortable if it means I walk away a rich bitch."

"We are kindred spirits, you and I." Alexis sighed. "If the red one is too much boob for you, then try the silver one!"

The silver dress was more modest than its red counterpart but lacked the white shawl underneath. Alexis shouted her approval after I twirled in it, and I began lacing it up the back. Or rather, I tried too. "They enchanted the damn wardrobe but not the dresses? It's impossible to tie the back by myself!"

"Well, don't look at me. The best I can do is cut it off you."

My efforts were interrupted by a soft knock at the door. "Ruby, I'm coming in." Lucca stepped into the room and paused. Amber eyes darkened into pools of desire as he took in the elegant dress hanging off my shoulders. He made his way over and took the laces from my struggling hands. "You look lovely."

I bit my lip, feeling my nipples harden as his long fingers moved softly against my skin. Each pull of fabric through the eyelets pricked at my senses until all I could focus on was the rush of sensation each time his touch traced along my back. Lucca drew closer and kissed my neck. I gasped, leaning my head to the side. Heat pooled in my lower belly as the demon ran his mouth along the juncture of my neck and shoulder. "So responsive." He murmured against my skin.

"You're not going to make this dinner easy for me, are you vixen? I'm going to have to sit through endless chatter while other men covet this body. Forgive me in advance if I pull you away early."

"Isn't the whole point of this week to show me off in front of them?" I asked breathlessly.

"No." His voice was rich and deep, reminiscent of a cello strung to perfection. Lucca spun me around and placed a searing kiss on my lips. His hand glided its way up the back of my neck before tilting my head, allowing him better access. His taste on my tongue was an aphrodisiac, blazing through my veins in a wicked promise of carnal delights. "It's to show them you're mine."

"F...For a week." I stammered.

"For a week." He conceded.

Spellbound and needy, I clung to his offered arm when he finally pulled away. I needed an anchor to stay upright, lest I fall flat on my face. "Steady now, vixen. We have a show to do."

Chapter 5

Lucca's kiss still had me reeling after we'd been seated in the dining hall. I sipped more of my cherry wine and tried to focus on the plate of roasted pheasant in front of me. All manner of wild game had been laid out on the long table. Boar, deer, pheasant, some weird mongoose-looking thing, the works - but all my lust-riddled mind could do was think about the man sitting next to me. To make matters worse, Lucca had been feeding me bites off his plate and using any excuse to keep his hands on me, which was the plan. Of course. But dammit, I was so horny!

"Don't look now, love. You've attracted yet another suitor."

My attention stayed glued to the plate, not bothering to check if he was right. I already knew by the way his knuckles traced along my thigh. Much like when we first arrived, the demons attending the feast took a keen interest in me. It hadn't been a full minute after I sat down that an overfly-friendly werewolf tried to offer me bites off his plate. Soon after, a man with moth wings and fuzzy antennas tried to regale me with tales of a fight against a squid beast. Anytime one of the men worked up the courage to approach, Lucca would see them off with a smirk and a possessive display of affection. The only guests not tripping over themselves were the dragon lord himself and the two other women at the table.

Well, one of the women did take an interest in me. But if her glare were any indication, I'd say it was more of searing hatred. Why I didn't know. She too had a small crowd of men trying to shove their way next to her. Lucca glanced at the pixie-faced woman, then brushed my hair behind my ear. "Don't mind her, love. Nydia isn't used to sharing the attention."

I took his hand in mine and kissed his knuckles. "It looks like she'd rather share a knife with my chest."

"As if I'd let anything happen to that bewitching chest."

"Bet my blade is bigger than hers." Alexis piqued up. The sword was hung over the back of my chair and had remained quiet for most of the feast. Her endless whining broke me down far enough that I agreed to bring her so long as she didn't cause trouble. Not that I'd ever admit it, but her presence gave me a sense of comfort. Being thrown into a magnificent castle with all manner of mythical creatures was exciting but also terrifying. A strong blade forged in my family's smithy gave me something to ground myself on - even if she never shut up.

At the head of the table sat the dragon lord and who I assumed was his wife. Each of them sported long dark green hair and a set of massive horns. The she-dragon was a heavyset, curvaceous woman that exuded feminine charm. When she stood to address the crowd, I could see that she towered over the average man.

"If I could have your attention for a moment," she began, tapping on her wine glass. "Herrick and I are so glad all of you came to join us for another Winter Festival. More importantly, the first Winter Festival since the end of Myva's rein of terror!" She raised her glass to the crowd, who responded in kind with loud cheers. I picked up my glass as well. If the ex-goddess killed off most of their women, then her death deserved a toast.

"Tonight, I say we dedicate this feast in honor of those brave heroes who risked their lives to free us all!" More cheers erupted from the crowd, and the she-dragon gave them a moment to settle down again. "As an extra special treat, the Shadow Dragon and his wife have graciously donated the ingredient responsible for lifting our curse. This cinnamon was the key ingredient to breaking the mind fog that held us captive. So now I'd like to share a taste of it with you all." She clapped her hands, and a flurry of little lizard men hurried out from the kitchen doors. They held trays with small silver bowls and began placing them in front of each guest.

"What are those?" I whispered.

"Kobolds," Lucca replied. "They're sprites capable of taking on the form of any small creature, and you'll usually find them working for powerful demons or playing tricks on mortals."

A red kobold the size of a raccoon stopped by my seat and placed one of the silver bowls in front of me. The tiny creature regarded me for a moment before smiling, little teeth poking out from his long jaw. *Adorable. In a small maid alligator sort of way.* I returned the friendly grin, and he scampered off to the next guest. The bowls contained a large portion of cinnamon and a spoon. I couldn't imagine the spice would taste very good on a pheasant, so I sliced off a small piece of wild boar and added it to my plate.

It was then I noticed the surrounding demons all taking a spoonful of cinnamon and raising it up. "To cinnamon!" Herrick boomed.

"To cinnamon!" the crowd roared back.

Frantically, I shot a hand out to stop Lucca from eating the powdered mistake. "Wait!" I shouted. "Everyone, hold on. You can't just eat it!" My warning came too late. As if time slowed, I watched in horror - and mild amusement - as everyone around me shoved a spoonful of cinnamon in their mouth.

The dragon lord himself was first to realize the error.

Herrick's eyes widened before he let out something between a cough and a wheeze. Plumes of cinnamon erupted from his mouth, then promptly ignited from flames shooting out his nose. The flaming spice ball caused the dragon to fall back out of his chair and hit the ground hard. Ragged coughs still lit up with burnt cinnamon as his guests followed his fate.

I tried not to laugh. I really did, but my willpower was no match for a snake man spitting spice out on a werebear. Laughter ripped out of my throat until my sides ached. Lucca, the only one I managed to save, wisely put down his spoonful.

"The dragon's clothes are on fire!" The sword announced before dissolving into a fit of giggles. Sure enough, our host had caught flame at some point, and the tiny lizard men swarmed the larger male to douse him with a pitcher of water.

Lucca threw back his head and laughed. "This is the greatest feast I've ever been to."

Across the table, Nydia turned a deep shade of red and shook her fist at me. "You stupid human! Why didn't you warn us this dust was poisonous?"

I wiped a tear from my face and tried to compose myself enough to answer. "It's not poisonous. You just can't eat it by the spoonful. I tried to warn you."

"Then why is Lucca the only one not wheezing?" She huffed. "For all we know, you could be another witch trying to trick us!"

Lucca glared at the woman. "That's a harsh accusation to be thrown at my mate. For your sake, I hope you have the proof to back it up."

"He's not coughing because I grabbed his hand. I didn't bring the cinnamon, lady. How would I even know you didn't understand how to eat it?" I stood from my chair and made a show of sprinkling more spice onto the boar meat then ate a large bite. "See? No coughing, no balls of fire."

Fat tears rolled down reddened Herrick's face. The dragon lord gave off another wheeze and slumped onto the table. His wheezing soon gave way to boisterous guffaws, and his body shook with the force of his hysterics. His wife succumbed to the same fit. She snorted loudly in-between giggles and through a hand in front of her face only to snort even louder.

Just like that, the room was filled with roaring laughter, and the dinner resumed. Nydia continued to shoot hateful glances my way, but I did my best to ignore her. It was hard to tell what kind of demon she was just by looking at her, but if I had to bet money at the time, I assumed it was one that could still kick my ass.

"Lucca," The dragoness called. She took a sip from her glass and sat back in her chair. "When are you going to introduce me to your guest? It's not often I get the pleasure of another woman's company."

Nydia's fork clinked against her plate as she took a stab at her meat, but the angry woman kept her head down.

The fox demon gave an easy grin and took my hand. "Where are my manners? Lady Camila, this is Ruby from the city of Goldcrest. Ruby, this is Lady Camila."

I inclined my head. "It's an honor ma'am."

Camila waved a hand in front of her face. "No need for the formalities dear. I'm thrilled to see you join us. I've never seen a human participate in the Doe Hunt before! Is that why you've brought your sword? Can't let these men win too easily can we?" She shimmied her shoulders and nudged her husband.

"Oh, are we deer hunting?" I asked.

Lucca cleared his throat and patted my hand. "We didn't plan on joining the hunt this year. Ruby and I are already together so I didn't see the point."

"We?" An orc spoke up. "*We* didn't plan on joining, or you didn't tell her? What's wrong, fox? Scared of a little competition?"

"Just because you're together doesn't mean you can't join the fun!" Camila huffed. "Herrick and I join in every year and we've been married for at least two hundred and thirty five years."

Burning hot metal flakes, how long do dragons live?

"Let her join in on the games ya jealous bastard!" Another man hollered.

I fiddled with the food on my plate, unsure of whether or not to speak up. "I like games. How do you play Doe Hunt?"

Lucca leaned an elbow on the table and rubbed his eyes. "Trust me, love, it's not a game you want to play."

At the head of the table, Camila clapped her hands together excitedly. "Oh hush you! She can decide if she wants. Now listen here Ruby, on the last day of the festival, we women take off into the mountain. After a good hour-long head start, the men set off to hunt us down!"

A chill went down my spine and my hands started to sweat.

"Then, once they catch up, the men will fight to see who gets to challenge us ladies." The dragoness' face was practically glowing. "If they defeat you in battle, then you spend the night together! It's such a romantic way to find a strong mate, don't you think?"

The table grew quiet. I peered around to see most of the men eagerly awaiting my answer. The answer was fuck no. "I um...I don't think I want to play that game. I'm not much of a fighter, so I doubt there will be much fun in challenging me."

The overly-friendly werewolf I'd met before laughed and pointed to Alexis.

"Oh don't be shy! You've got a sword with you. I'm sure you could put up a decent fight if you wanted."

"I'm a blacksmith," I said, shrugging. "The sword is basically product placement." Alexis snickered behind me, but I ignored her.

Lucca took my hand and gave it a comforting squeeze. "You don't have to participate if you don't want to."

Nydia scoffed and folded her arms. "Let her run off home then. The little human probably thinks the Doe Hunt is for barbarians."

The grip on my hand tightened. Lucca fixed the woman with a steely glare and she shifted uncomfortably in her seat.

"Maybe Nydia has a point." Camila sighed. She brought a fist to her chin and hummed. "Perhaps our game is a bit too dangerous for humans. If we're going to live amongst them again, we should think about altering the game to be more inclusive." She turned back to me and smiled. "Are there any winter activities that humans have?"

I rubbed the back of my neck and thought for a moment. "Well, we usually deck the city in boughs of holly. Hang mistletoe to kiss under and bake cookies-"

"That's it!" Camila shouted.

"What, the cookies?" I asked.

"No, no. You said you hang mistletoe to kiss under right? What if we sent you off with some mistletoe of your own, and whoever takes it from you wins! You won't have to fight if you don't want to, you can just give the mistletoe to whoever catches you first."

"You hear that fox? Once I'm done kicking your ass, her mistletoe is as good as mine." The orc taunted.

Lucca swirled his glass and refused to look at him. "I could be fevered and drunk and still never lose a fight to you, Matuk. Do yourself a favor and just give up now."

The dragoness clapped excitedly, her voice bubbling in glee. "Oh this is so exciting! Our first hunt with a human. We could call it Mistlefoe! Oh please say you'll join in, Ruby!"

"I...guess that sounds alright." Camila hollered and began chatting about past hunts. Most of it seemed terrifying to be a part of, but I guessed demon women were built with harder stuff.

After a long time, the first brave guest got up and excused themselves, giving the rest of us social cowards an opening to leave as well. Lucca stood, offering me his arm, and I grasped it and gave a polite wave to our hosts on the way out. "If you don't mind, I'd like to show you another area of the castle."

"So long as no one else tries to spoon feed me pheasant."

A grin tugged at the corner of his lips, and he shook his head. "The place I have in mind is a little more private, or at least it should be. You never know what sort of dastardly Kraken has hidden in the shadows, ready to swoop in and feed you all manner of terrors."

"The painting you just put in my mind…" I drawled.

My demon slung an arm lazily around my waist and led us down a long corridor. I leaned into his touch and took in his masculine scent. He smelled like pine trees and moonlight…and there was something else…a heady, soothing essence similar to stargazer lilies. The beautiful white and pink flower suited him. Both gave off a wild yet refined demeanor, and you couldn't help but get lost in them.

Our stroll ended when Lucca stopped in front of an arched doorway. Steam pooled from the outside once he opened the door and let me inside. "Sweet golden ores, it's a hot spring!" I said. The steam cleared from my vision, revealing the treasure hidden in the mountainside. Pools of moonlit water were scattered along the open area, separated by blue-green moss. The center held one massive pool connected to a waterfall coming off the side of a cliff. The springs closest to the castle walls were shielded by white curtains strung over golden arches.

I suddenly felt all too aware of the sweat and grime I'd gathered throughout the day. A hot bath sounded like absolute bliss. Or it would if it were private. Other guests must have shared Lucca's thoughts and were happily relaxing away…and they were naked. Nudity must not have been a big deal to demons, as none of the bathers felt the need to cover themselves when we walked in. Most of the men were spread out in the main bath, while the larger, more beast-like demons took up individual pools. One lamia had stretched its long snake body along the rock lining of a larger spring, half dipped into the inviting water.

I followed Lucca into one of the shielded springs along the wall. I let out a breath of relief that he didn't expect me to bathe out in the open. The tented room simply held a stone bench and a small spring. Light orange flowers climbed up the wall of the castle on their dark vines, adding just a pop of color to the room. "Wait here, Vixen. I'll be back in a moment with a few towels."

"Take your time. You'll have to drag me out of this bath." I said before setting Alexis down.

"Don't tempt me, woman." Lucca disappeared behind the curtain and I was left alone.

Quickly, I shed the dress and lowered myself into the water's intoxicating warmth. "Oh, gods that's nice." I sighed. Wars could be solved with baths. I was sure of it. Resting my head back on the stone wall, I sank further into the water and rested my eyes.

Footsteps near the door cut that rest short. "Back already Lucca?"

The figure's silhouette pulled back the curtain and stepped inside. "Guess again you little rat."

"Great, what's this bitch doing here?" Alexis asked from the place behind me.

Nydia's small face contorted into a scowl. She flicked her honey-colored hair back and drew closer. "What the hell did you just say to me, human?"

Chapter 6

"I didn't say anything-"

"To you." Alexis finished for me. "If I wanted to waste my time talking to a selfish little whelp incapable of grasping their own insignificance in this world, I'd get a cat."

This damn sword is trying to get me killed!

"What are you doing?" I hissed at Alexis.

"In here?" She finished for me again.

Dread seeped through my bones as Nydia's hands grew to claws. The steam in the room must have been obscuring my face, letting her think Alexis was speaking for me. "I'm here to tell you to stay away from Lucca, you ugly little shit!"

"Why so you can add him back into your harem of 'please gods, someone give the attention my daddy never did?'"

"Whoa!" I yelled in disbelief. I knew the sword was literally made to antagonize the people around her, but damn. She cut to the heart and wasn't even out of her sheath.

"Whoa, wowee and boohoo. Why is this simmering pile of insecurity still in my damn bath?" The sword shot back.

Nydia looked ready to skin me alive. She bent forwards and a snarl broke from her throat. The simple white gown she wore split down the back, revealing honey-shaded fur. In a flash, the petite woman was gone, and pissed off looking werecat stood in her place. "I will rip the flesh from your bones-"

"And give them to Lucca so he can see how psycho you are? Go ahead, fashion my femur into a little heart-shaped bracelet, and put it on his pillow as a gift, you hopeless stalker. Men love that."

The werecat's eyes widened. After a small breath, she lowered her claws, but still bared her fangs. "I don't even need to kill you! I'm just here to give you a warning. Stay away from my men. Every man on this mountain belongs to me."

"Sweetheart, the only thing you're giving is desperation. We get it, you were the golden girl. Some even might say an era, but the era has ended."

"You are just begging me to rip you apart!" Nydia roared.

I raised my hands up in surrender. "No, I'm not!"

"The only thing I'm begging you to do is keep talking, so I have a reason to let *your man* get *me* pregnant just to make you suffer. Ever see a human bring a living, breathing creature into this world out of spite? Cause you're about to."

Nydia's, and my mouth fell open. She stood there wide-eyed for a moment before huffing out a breath. "Whatever. We'll see just how soon Lucca comes to his senses and drops you!" With that, she turned around and stalked out of the room.

"I'll see you at the wedding darling!" Alexis made kissing noises at the departing werecat. Once Nydia was out of sight, her voice dropped low, irritation dripping from her words. "Ruby, I'm going to need to take one for the team and marry that fox for real.

"What is wrong with you?"

"A lot of things. But what's important right now, is that we never let Lucca go back to her. My pride won't allow it. I don't have a body to distract him, so you're going to have to push those tits up and show him what we're working with."

"You are impossible. Start a fight like that again, and I'll throw you into the snow to rust."

"You'd miss me." She snorted.

Groaning, I sank back into the bath. "I'm ignoring you." There was a good chance Nydia would try her luck again. She didn't seem like the type to give up easily. As far as crazy ex-girlfriends went, this one was sure to be a pain in the ass.

Gentle ripples of water eased the tension in my muscles. I focused on their smooth rhythm, willing away any thoughts of Lucca and Nydia together. The image left a foul taste in my mouth - but I tried to tell myself it didn't matter. *I'm just here for a week. I have no reason to be thinking of who that man spends his time with. The only thing I have to do is sit back and enjoy being pampered, just like he promised - and make sure a wearcat doesn't stab me in my sleep.*

The man in question finally reappeared, carrying towels and more wine. "You offer me a mine, fluffy towels, and booze? Lucca, I'm starting to think you're a figment of my imagination."

He grinned and set his load down near the bath. "Is that your way of saying you'll dream of me?"

"I guess we'll find out tonight, won't we?" I taunted. The white scarf around his neck twitched, then fell off him to swing behind his lower back.

Oh it's his tail!

"Hmm," he murmured. "That sounds an awful lot like a challenge." With slow, deliberate movements, Lucca un-fashioned the ties of his pants and the great tail discovery was wiped clean from my mind. Breathing suddenly became more difficult as I watched his hands work. The tanned leather of his belt was tossed away, letting the offensive garment sag lower on his hips. Its absence divulged a tantalizing hint of umber skin.

His thumb toyed with the hem of the garment, sliding across the waistband. I swallowed and shifted in my spot in the water. A dull throb ached in my pussy and every shred of my thoughts was held captive by the way his thumb dipped into the waist of his pants. He pulled them down just a breath. It was just enough to tease the dip of his hipbone before he removed his hand entirely.

By sheer force of will, I forced down the groan that threatened to give away my desperation. I'd known this man for a day, and yet I never wanted to taste something as badly as I wanted the dip of his hip. I wanted to touch his warm, dark skin, wanted to rip his clothes off and drag my tongue along the hard planes of his chest. I wanted to taste him till I sated the alarming infatuation I didn't want to feel after such a short time.

The rational part of me wanted to step back and collect myself. Figure out the best plan of action for handling my incessant want for him, without getting lost in him. But then I was seized in molten eyes of amber, and I knew: I was already gone.

Standing up out of the water, I made my way to the edge of the pool and stopped in front of Lucca. There, at the edge, I could make out his faint scent. Intoxicating and male, it rose just above the smell of soaps and incense that paraded the bath. Giving into my body's need, I traced my knuckles against his bare skin. "Aren't you going to join me?"

"Vixen," he rumbled. "Are you certain you want what happens if I do?"

He was so close. So achingly close that I found myself leaning forward, and running my tongue along his hip. *Fucking. Bliss.*

"I do."

My demon gave off a strangled cry, then shed the rest of his clothing in a hurry. "I'm sorry," He rasped, rushing into the water. His mouth clamped over mine and began to kiss me as if our hearts would stop if he didn't. I moaned into his touch and he took the advantage to delve into my mouth. The tip of his tongue danced against my own as his hands molded me against him.

Yes, gods, he fits against me so perfectly.

"I meant to take my time with you." He whispered, nipping at my lip. Heat rushed through my body as I felt his mouth trail along the fragile arch of my throat. "Meant to have you waking to my tongue on your cunt each morning…until you grew wet at just the sight of me before I had you." His hard length pressed against my thigh and my hips jerked. "But how am I supposed to resist you like this? Tell me vixen and I'll stop. If you don't then I'll spread your legs right here in this bath where everyone can hear you scream. Damn it all, Vixen. I want them to hear, I want every man on this fucking mountain to know whose cock you're coming on."

"Isn't that the whole point?"

He chuckled against my neck. "I think I might love you." He chased a hand under my thigh and lifted my ass until I wrapped myself around him. He moved us to a shallower end of the water before resting me down on a smooth rock. "Stay here." He murmured. "Don't move."

My belly quivered under his lips and I gave a small nod of compliance. Lucca retreated to fetch the wine he'd brought and returned just as quick. The fog in the room had hampered my vision, but I got the feeling the fox demon had no such issues - not with the way his eyes glowed golden in the mist. They ran up my body, seeming to map out every curve and dip as if it were his own hands touching me. I spotted a white flash of teeth and heard a pop and then he filled a glass of wine, setting it down next to me with the bottle.

"Just one glass?" I asked.

"I've found something better." He sank himself In between my legs and kissed the portion of my knee that was still above water. My throat went dry and he lowered his head underwater to trail his tongue along my inner thigh.

"Lucca wait!"

The demon paused his exploration to lift his head and looked at me. For whatever reason, the sight of that beautiful creature between my legs made me feel a rush of self-consciousness. He'd already gone down on me once and I'd yet to reciprocate anything. It was hard enough getting most men I'd dated to go down there at all.

"You…don't have to do that. I'm ready enough. Or, why don't I give you a turn?" I went to sit up, but he firmly held me in place.

He cocked his head and his brows furrowed. "Vixen…who taught you to think that way?" he dragged a finger up my thigh, making me shudder. "Was it the human men at the bottom of the mountain? They must not have understood the gift in front of them, how to treat your juicy little cunt." He sighed and shook his head as if disappointed. "Don't fret, love. I have you now."

My back arched as he traced the slit of my pussy. "Lucca, I just-"

"You're just going to lie back and drink your wine while I eat you. I've been waiting all day to taste you like a peach. Hours of mulling through that damn feast, knowing my dessert was just out of reach. I'm going to savor you like the very first fruit of Spring and you'll see just what a patient man I've been."

The glass shook as I brought it to my face. It took a moment to steady myself long enough to take a sip, but I did. Swallowing down the sweet liquid at his request.

A slow grin spread on the demon's lips. "That's better," he murmured before his head slipped beneath the water once more. His tongue slid up my aching folds before flicking over my clit. He circled the tiny bud with a firm pressure that had my toes curling.

My eyelashes fluttered closed. "Oh gods." He toyed with me for a minute, that wicked tongue running along the dip of my core. He pushed the tip of his tongue inside before drawing out again to give another long lick. Whimpering, I hooked my legs around his shoulders, silently willing him to go further. I felt him smile against me, and his hands curved around my ass before he grabbed hold and delved his tongue inside my pussy.

Wine sloshed out of the cup as I jerked against him. "Oh," I breathed. "Oh fuck!" I had just enough sense left to set the glass down before my legs convulsed around him. He gave a rough flick against my clit and I damn near came undone. My hand slapped over my mouth muffling a guttural moan.

Water lapped against the stone wall in time with the frantic jerk of my hips. The sound melded with the breathless pants and little pleas on my lips. Lucca slid his fingers inside me, immediately recalling the location of that sweet spot. The slap of the water became timed to the thrust of his fingers and I locked onto the sound like a mantra. Each slap was followed by the shock of pleasure as he hit that spot just...*right.* He alternated long licks and flicks of his tongue, while his fingers continued their work of rubbing my throbbing pussy. He fucked me with his lips and tongue, tasting me, feasting on me like a starving man.

I bit my knuckle to keep from crying out and alerting the other guests. It worked...for a moment. But then he took my clit into his mouth and sucked hard.

My body spasmed. Electrifying white-hot pleasure shot across my vision. Something between a yelp and a groan cut over the sound of waves and I dug my heels into the demon's back. After the first rolling wave of pleasure hit, I spilled out Lucca's name like a prayer, again and again as I helplessly jerked my hips against his mouth. Butterflies danced in my spasming stomach as he kept up his pace, sending tears to my eyes when my orgasm seemed to go on and on forever.

Finally, he came up for air and released me. The after-waves of my release had me shaking as he pulled me to him. His lips traced along my collarbone as he panted. "How are you so fucking sweet, Vixen?"

"Just...just lucky I guess."

His mouth twitched up in a smile. Water streamed down his white hair, plastering it to his face, and framing his sharp features. In the dim light of our somewhat private room, I saw him for the monster he was. Not the kind we initially feared the demons would be back in the city. This was much worse. Lucca was temptation incarnate. Beautiful, feral, corrupt. This was a creature that whisked away women in the dead of the night, never to be seen again - because they'd never agree to leave.

He glanced off behind me before the grin on his face turned into something almost sinister. I gasped in surprise when he suddenly lifted me. Quickly, I wrapped my arms around his shoulders as he stepped out of the water and sat down on end of the bench. He settled me on his lap, his thick cock sliding up against my lower belly. Then he pressed his lips to the curve of my ear and whispered. "My irresistible little vixen. Look at the crowd you've drawn."

"Crowd?" I looked around lazily, my mind was still fogged from the after-effects of release. Movement beyond the curtain finally caught my eye. The first figure I noticed was a hulking man, probably an orc. He was hunched over, hand on his crotch as he scurried out to the hot springs. The main bath was suspiciously empty, yet each pool closest to ours suddenly held far more guests than I'd seen when we first walked in. *They were watching us.* Judging by the suggestive sounds coming from the tent next to us, some were doing a little more than watching.

The reason for Lucca's change in position clicked in my head. With my ass firmly seated in his lap, and arms draped around his neck, our silhouette must have created quite the implication. My demon wanted to give them a show. The idea sent a thrill of something new and empowering through my soul. *Why shouldn't we? It was the reason I was here.* "Kiss me," I demanded.

He groaned and covered my mouth with his, nipping at my lower lip until I opened for him. He slid his tongue along mine, making me delirious with need once more. My nipples scraped deliciously against his chest as he lifted me up. Lucca's fingers dug into my ass and my breath hitched as I felt his cock press against my core. "Yes." I moaned. It should have felt taboo, maybe it was. But the fact that the men behind the curtain were about to see me get taken by my demon for the first time made me feel desired and sexy. It was something hard to feel when I was just the girl who ran the blacksmith shop. But here I didn't have to worry about that. Here my arms weren't too muscular, here my blunt nature wasn't too off-putting. No, here I was a temptress claiming her mate.

And Lucca...Lucca was *intoxicating*. He ran his tongue on my breasts and began to push into me. My breath came out in a needy whine as I stretched to accommodate him, stroking and petting at his shoulders and hair as he worked inside me inch by fucking inch. The slight upward curve of his dick pushed him right against the sweet spot I craved. *Of course, he'd have the perfect dick for me too. It simply wasn't fair.*

"Yes, my sweet Ruby. Take all of me, I know you can." he lavished my chest before driving his hips up, seating me completely on his cock. I clung to him as he thrust again, and again, trying my best to match his thrusts against my sweet spot.

"Lucca," I panted. "More. Fuck, please, I need more!"

"Yes," he hissed against my shoulder. His nails dug into the meat of my ass and he ground me down hard. "Anything you like, Vixen." my eyes all but rolled into the back of my head at the intense pleasure the friction was giving me. My nails scraped against his back and he cried out. So I did it again, earning me an even more frantic pace. Lucca drove into me like a man possessed, green swirls of mist mixed in with the steam until the whites of the sheets faded away into a field of endless wildflowers.

Something seemed to snap in him then. I yelped as the field swirled around me. Before I could catch my breath, I was on my back, helplessly pinned beneath Lucca. Vines from the wildflowers shot out to bind my hands above my head, while a soft moss-covered stump formed beneath my ass, lifting me higher, the vines wrapped around my thighs and lifted them towards my chest, trapping me open for him as the fox demon drove deeper.

If I thought I was near death earlier in the snow, I must have eloped with him then. I threw back my head and cried out in jumbled moans, arching and bucking under him.

"You're mine," Lucca growled, sinking in again. His hand dug into my hair as he repeated the word with each thrust. "Mine, mine, mine."

I looked between us to see a rose of some sort winding its way toward my clit. The impossibly soft rose petals enclosed around the soft bud and-

"OH, SWEET GODS ALMIGHTY." I might have blacked out, I might have died. Honestly, I wasn't sure. But if the vines weren't holding me in place for him, there was a good chance I would have levitated off the ground. Excellent planning on his part.

Lucca grunted and continued his pace, and that dangerous rose continued to work my clit. I felt his cock begin to pulse, and that damn rose sent off a vibrating sensation that sent me over the edge in record time. Lucca's body seized as my walls clamped down around him, and he shuddered out his release. He ground his cock deep inside me before collapsing. The vines and stump receded as he rolled onto his side, tucking me firmly against him.

We just laid there for a while. Boneless and panting and trying to remember important things like names and our current location. Eventually, the flowers faded into sheets and stone once more.

"Did I win then?" Lucca asked.

"Win what?"

"Will you dream of me?"

I threw my arm over my eyes, too tired to even feel embarrassed. "Sweetheart, I don't know if I can dream anymore. I'm a broken woman."

He let out a breathless laugh and pulled me closer.

"I don't even know my name. I don't even know anything. I just know I need a nap. Take your win. I don't care."

"Oh, I intend to, Ruby."

Chapter 7

The following few days were a pleasant whirlwind of good food, good company, and general dick wizardry. Lucca and I fell into a simple rhythm of flirting in front of guests and spending our time lazing in the hot springs or exploring the castle. It still felt strangely intimate to share a bed with him, but I was usually so bone-tired from well...*boning* that sleep came instantly and I was spared the awkwardness of trying to figure out where to put my arms or whether I snored in his ear.

My paradise had only one major flaw: It was ending. And I really, really didn't want it to. The thought of saying goodbye to Lucca gnawed at my chest.

"Just tell him you're in love with him, dammit." Alexis snapped.

My paradise had two flaws. It was ending, and that damn sword. "It's not that simple." I said, groaning into my pillow.

She huffed and rattled a little in her sheath. "Oh or it is, and you're just overthinking it. What's the problem? And don't give me that 'It's too soon' bullshit. You two have been swooning over each other like lost puppies since you met."

"That's the problem! What if it's just an act for him? What if I'm the only one having trouble pretending?" It was all fun and games at the start - as well as a great excuse to explore the intense sexual chemistry I had with Lucca. But now, when he pulled me in for a kiss at the dinner table, my stomach flipped and my knees grew weak. *Stupid emotions. They ruin everything.*

"Wow," the sword gasped. "I never thought of it like that. But you know, there is one sure-fire way to solve this."

"How?"

"You use your fucking words and ask him."

"Ask me what?" Lucca's deep voice made me jump up, nearly falling off the bed. I scrambled upright to see him standing in the doorway with a tray of food. *Of course, he brought me breakfast in bed. This agent of heart chaos.*

"Ruby caught feelings and wants to know if you think she'd look good with a baby bump."

"Alexis!" I hissed.

"Yes." He said simply, before setting the tray down on the nightstand.

I blinked. "I'm sorry, what?"

The demon moved to the bed and ran his hands gently across my thighs. My breath hitched as he grabbed my ass and pulled me to the edge. Kneeling, he spread my legs in front of him and toyed with the hem of my pants. "Do you want one now?"

Words jumbled and died in my throat. The beat of my heart pounded away in my ears as Lucca awaited my answer. "I…you…are you serious? We barely know each other."

He hummed. "You're right. I'll want a good year or two with you to myself first."

"Lucca I'm serious."

"As am I. If you want to learn more about me first, then fine. I'll answer any questions you want - but I won't pretend a week with you will be enough for me. I like you far too much." He sat back on the bed and pulled me into his arms. "In time, maybe you'll even get over your aversion to sleeping in the same bed."

"You knew about that?" I squawked, heat racing across my cheeks.

He chucked and rested his head on my shoulder. "Alexis told me."

I glared at the hunk of junk, who was suddenly quiet as a mouse."

"And you don't snore." He continued. "You talk."

"No I don't!"

"Last night you took me through the delicate process of creating claymores. Although, I'd have to say my favorite line has been 'Rob's paper juice.' Please tell me if that actually has any meaning. I'm dying to know."

I buried my face in my hands. "I'm not hearing this. You are full of lies."

"Maybe. But I'm not lying about wanting more time with you. I was honestly hoping your father would try something stupid, so I had an excuse to extend the curse and keep you longer."

I did my best to keep my voice stern, ignoring the giddy happiness creeping into my dead heart. "If this is going to work, you need to stop putting curses on my family."

"...a little curse?"

"Lucca."

"Fine." He sighed. "Just agree to be mine."

Leaning back against him, I took in the comforting warmth his body provided. "You aren't concerned with this whole thing moving too fast?"

He shrugged. "So what if it is? Being with you these past few days has been bliss. Maybe it will work out and we'll grow old and gray together. Or maybe it will end in heartbreak. If it's the latter then...well I know of a cliff on the east side of my territory that would be great for brooding off into the night."

I laughed, the nervous tension in my shoulders easing just a bit. "You make it sound so easy."

"Sometimes it is." He kissed my temple and traced small circles on the back of my hand. Warmth spread from my head down to my toes at the small, sweet gesture. Even just sitting together like this felt so right. If the ache in my chest wasn't love, it was damn close.

"Just say yes, vixen."

Fuck it. "Yes."

Lucca pulled me in for a kiss. A gentle meeting of lips far tamer than the ravenous hunger we'd been showing each other just the night before - but it felt deeper. It was filled with more passion than I thought possible.

The sound of sniffling broke through the room. "My heart is so full right now." Alexis whimpered.

I broke the kiss and let my head fall on his shoulder. "Dammit."

"I'm sorry." She sniffed. "Just ignore me. Gods, I love a happy ending."

"Alright, I'm breaking the curse early." Lucca said, raising his hand.

"Wait, come on!" The sword hollered. "You can't do this to your old pal! Your old buddy Alexis! You two would still be dancing around each other if it wasn't for me. I demand excusal from all curse removals."

I laughed and placed my hand on Lucca's wrist. "She has a point. I'm fine with one talking sword."

"I knew you'd come around! After this festival, I say we still blow this joint and go to the beach! Fox boy can come too…I guess."

"So honored to be included." Lucca said, a wry grin playing on his face. He snapped his fingers, and I felt a small pulse of energy shoot through the room. "There, sword excluded, your father's curse has been lifted."

"So what happens now?" I asked.

"I've already met with the dragon lord and gotten my approval for my territory. All that's left is the hunt tomorrow. Unless you wanted to leave early?"

"I feel like Lady Camila would cry a river if I did." I cursed my weakness for peer pressure. The woman looked awfully happy, and I'd been staying at her home, eating her food and banging in her hot-springs. The least I could do was humor her in a game. With her changing the rules to accommodate humans, I thought it wouldn't be too bad. "One more day won't kill me. Just make sure you're the one to catch up to me first. I don't want to go kissing some stranger."

Lucca chuckled, pulling me closer. "Wouldn't dream of it, Vixen. When you and the other women head out in the morning, just head east to the large cherry tree nestled in the valley. I'll meet you there."

"Sounds like cheating." I teased.

"Did you want to kiss a Spitaur?"

"Nope. Never mind, cheating is great. I'll be good."

"I thought so."

Chapter 8

Peer pressure could go suck a dick. This mountain, this game, Nydia, the direction East, all of them could go suck a dick. My lungs burned as I pushed myself faster back up the mountain slope. Shooting pain from my calves reiterated the fact that I was wildly out of shape - but when you're being chased by literal nightmares, stopping wasn't really an option.

"Swing me left!" Alexis shouted. I screamed and swung wide, barely catching a shot of web before it latched onto me. The mistletoe hanging from her handle brushed against my hands, flinging snowflakes into the air. Behind me, the spitaur cursed. He and the two minotaur chasing me had nearly caught up. My only hope of getting away was climbing over a ridiculously prominent ridge, hoping I'd finally get to the cherry tree where I was supposed to meet Lucca. "I thought you said the sun rose in the West?"

I growled and heaved my exhausted body up over a boulder. "I said the sun rose in either the East or the West! There are only four directions. I figured a fifty-fifty shot was better than none!"

"Tell that to daddy eight legs and the bull brigade!" She snapped.

"Why couldn't he curse you to shoot fire or something?"

"Swing right!"

"Arg!" Arms screaming, I swung and caught the lighter-colored minotaur by the horn. Steel struck keratin and sent him crashing backwards into the spitaur. Together they fell back and rolled down the ridge before crashing into a tree. Chest heaving, I slumped against the ledge and held my hand up to the remaining minotaur. "Can we take a break? Please." I said, gasping for air. "I'm so tired, just…go after Nydia or something."

The shaggy brown bull climbed on top of a boulder not too far below where I rested. Where I was fighting for my life just to breathe, he looked like he just left for a stroll. *Damn demons and their crazy endurance.*

"Now why would I do that when I'm about to have a pretty woman all to myself for a night?" His words were spoken in a soft, flirtatious manner, but the ever-increasing bulge in his pants changed his tone to more of a threat. Judging by the size, I guessed the 'bull' part of a minotaur extended past the head and hooves. It was possible there was some brave woman out there that would happily step up to his challenge, but I was not that bitch.

"Well, you know I'm already with Lucca. Game or no, I plan on spending my night with him."

He snorted and continued to climb. I groaned and resumed my mad dash over the ledge. "That's not what Nydia said. She told us all this morning how you and that fox split up."

I'd been hearing a lot of that. As soon as my hour head start was over, I'd been bombarded with demons trying their luck. All of them had been told the same lie of my single lady status. If I ever got my hands on that cat, I'd throttle her.

By sheer force of luck, I'd lost most of my pursuers after a landslide separated them from my path. Unfortunately the remaining three were a hardy bunch. "I don't know what you're talking about! Lucca and I are still very much together. That woman is a liar and a charlatan!"

"Don't worry, little human. One night with me and you'll see I can treat you much better than him."

Or break my back in half. Pulling myself up to the top, I slumped over and cast a glance at the minotaur. "Please listen to me. Look at my mouth words. I am not single. Lucca and I are still together. Please leave me be!"

"If that's true, then why hasn't he come for you?"

"Because I'm dumb and didn't know which direction fucking East is!" My screaming carried over the mountain, causing an echo. It rang with the increasing fury I'd been feeling all morning. When the echo rang a third time, the trees scattered around us started to shake.

The bull looked around at the shifting foliage and backed himself against the ledge. I peered over the other side of the ledge to see a half-dead bush tremble and twist. Its limbs sprung to life and grew rapidly to form a sled. If it wasn't so damn cold, I would have bawled my eyes out at the sight. Without a second thought, I jumped on the sled and cut the branch, keeping it in place. It shot down the mountainside at a breakneck pace. An icy wind whipped at my face, but I didn't care. In the distance, I could see the bright pink outline of a cherry tree and I was headed straight for it. The sled was whipped forward by passing branches before coming to a stop near my destination.

There, under the beautiful falling cherry blossoms, stood Lucca in all his glory. And that bitch wasn't far behind him. When Nydia caught sight of my approach, she attempted to grab Lucca's arm, batting her eyelashes. He immediately shook her off and rushed to my side. "Vixen, thank the gods you're alright." He scooped me up from the sled and ran a warm hand over my cheeks. "You're freezing!"

Shivering with cold and rage, I pushed away from him and snatched the mistletoe off Alexis's handle. "Hold this." Shoving the plant into his hands, I stomped over to the cat demon.

She sneered and crossed her arms. "You're too late, I've already decided I'm going to let Lucca win my ch-"

Her face met my fist as I cocked back, swung, and rocked her shit to the ground. Nydia went down hard and I kicked her for good measure. Still seething, I shook my fist in her face. "Don't you ever, ever make me run again!"

"What are you talking about, and where have you been?" Lucca asked.

Alexis let out an exasperated sigh. "The cat bitch told everyone you two broke up last night. We've been fighting tooth and nail all morning to keep other men from taking our mistletoe. A lot of running was involved. It was terrible."

"Oh, you arrogant little brat!" Nydia whipped a trail of blood from her chin and leaped to her feet. In a flash, she transformed into a werecat and lunged.

I stumbled back, but her claws never met their mark. Roots of the cherry tree sprung up to wrap around her legs. She hissed and struggled, but the roots only grew higher, wrapping around her body from head to toe. The cat demon growled in frustration but suddenly stopped dead. Her face paled as she looked behind me.

Lucca pushed me behind him. "You knowingly put Ruby in danger just because you couldn't stomach the thought of me looking at anyone else. I should kill you for this."

"You can't truly choose a human over me?" She hissed. "I'm stronger than she could ever be! I won't lose you or anyone else to those sniffling little bottom dwellers."

"Nydia, you are not even an option. I'd still choose Ruby or a thousand demons because I'm in love with her."

"He said the L-word." The sword whispered beneath her sheath.

"It doesn't matter what you do, that fact will never change. She is the one I want to be with until the moment I stop breathing, and until I can find her again in the next life. She is my soulmate and if you ever even think of getting in the way of that again, it will be the last mistake you ever make."

Lucca turned to face me, and my heart set off like the wheels of a racing chariot. "I love you Ruby, I love you so fucking much and don't you dare tell me it's too soon. I know you feel this too."

Tears pricked the corners of my eyes. "I love you too."

Lucca removed his coat and wrapped it around my shoulders, and kissed me deeply. "Even half-frozen, you're still too sweet for your own good."

"I guess you'll just have to find a way to warm me up, won't you?"

He flashed a grin and pulled me closer. "I bet I can think of something."

"Gods, I hope it's that thing with the rose."

Acknowledgments

Thank you, Alexis, Blair, Kiran, Ashley, Rebekah, and Sabrina. You ladies gave me the courage to change everything and try something new, and I hope you know how much that means to me. You are without a shadow of a doubt, some of the best friends I've ever had.

Special thanks to the Mocks and Cocks book club, for preaching the word of my debut novel That Time I Got Drunk And Saved A Demon. Its success would not have been possible without you.

To my family, whom I've specifically asked not to read my smutty books; I love you, but I'm blocking you on social media.

About the Author

Kimberly Lemming is on an eternal quest to avoid her calling as a main character. She can be found giving the slip to that new werewolf that just blew into town and refusing to make eye contact with a prince of a far-off land. Dodging aliens looking for Earth booty can really take up a girl's time.

But when she's not running from fate, she can be found writing diverse fantasy romance. Or just shoveling chocolate in her maw until she passes out on the couch.

You can connect with me on:

- https://www.kimberlylemming.com
- https://twitter.com/KimberlyLemming
- https://www.facebook.com/KimberlyLemming
- https://www.instagram.com/kimberlylemming
- https://www.tiktok.com/@kimberlylemming

Subscribe to my newsletter:

✉ https://www.kimberlylemming.com/newsletter

Also by Kimberly Lemming

That Time I Got Drunk And Saved A Demon (Mead Mishaps Book 1)

All I wanted to do was live my life in peace. Maybe get a cat, expand my spice farm. Really, anything that doesn't involve going on a quest where an orc might rip my face off. But they say the Goddess has favorites. If so, I'm clearly not one of them.

After saving the demon Fallon in a wine-drunk stupor, all he wanted to do was kill an evil witch enslaving his people.

I mean, I get it, don't get me wrong. But he's dragging me along for the ride, and I'm kind of peeved about it. On the bright side, he keeps burning off his shirt.

Printed in Great Britain
by Amazon

10170834R00037